MOLLY AND THE BULLY

The Daily Rounds of a Hound Series

BOOK TWO

Written by Ed Payne   Illustrated by Britt Sekulić

DEDICATION

This book is dedicated to my family -- my wife Laura,
my daughters Ellyce and Corynne, and my mom Carolynn --
who have supported me at every turn. I also give a special
salute to Corynne who helped inspire this story by
overcoming middle school bullying to thrive in high school.

-- Ed

I dedicate this book to all the little ones far and wide.
May this story bring smiles to your faces and help you
learn a thing or two.

-Britt

Have you met our hound Molly?
A hound about town.
A hound most profound.

Do you know Molly's story?
Have you heard it before?
She comes from a shelter.
But there's a whole lot more.

It was simple at first.
Molly gets a new home.
She gets a new life.
She gets a new family.
But there's a bit of strife.

There were puppies on board,
Something she neglected to tell us.

Things worked out fine
(but you know, folks can be jealous)

When you're the new hound in town,
the word gets around.
And the local dogs think
They can put you down.

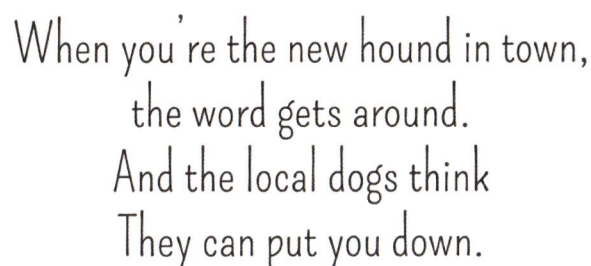

Molly's pups took the brunt.
The neighbor dogs were quite blunt.

Then came the cruelest moment of all.
One that hit the pups like a bowling ball.

A chihuahua named Charlee
thought she knew what was best.
She picked out the littlest pup - Patches
and put him to the test.

"You're nothing but a mutt,"
she snarled.
"I'm going to bite you in the ... tail."
Charlee growled,
and the little pups howled
It scared Patches so,
that he just wailed.

WAA!

The neighbor dogs laughed,
convinced it was funny.
"Go away," they said.
"Now run like a bunny."

Whimpering and whining,
Patches ran straight home.
The other pups followed.
Molly said "You're not alone."

In Patches heart, he was hurting.
He couldn't help who he was,
what he looked like,
or where he came from.

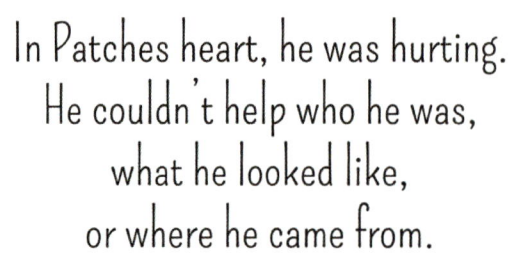

Molly knows the pain.
All shelter dogs do.
She was lost, then was found.
So goes the life of the hound.

But the streets can be tough.
And sometimes,
just a tad bit rough.

During that time
Molly learned a lesson of value.
It's when she was homeless,
and in need of rescue.

You see pit bulls like Frederick
have a bad reputation.
People judge them first,
but they're often mistaken.

Some call them bullies,
still that's not quite fair.
But Frederick rose above it,
he had something to share.

"Love," Frederick told Molly,
"is the key to it all."
"They can scorn you."
"They can hate you."
"But it's up to you,
to love one and all."

Then Frederick was gone.
The streets are that way.
Hounds come and go.
But his message
would stay.

It was Frederick's story
Molly shared with the pups.
A story to prepare them
for what would come up.

When the little hounds went out next,
guess who was waiting?
It was Charlee of course.
And there was all sorts of hating.

She was snarling.
She was snapping.
She just wouldn't stop yapping.
"You're nothing but mutts," Charlee sneered.
"I'm going to bite you in the ..."

But the pups had an answer.
One they made quite clear.
"Stop right there," Patches said,
as Molly's little hounds joined in chorus.
"We love you, Charlee,
and we don't care if you ignore us."

Charlee stopped in her tracks.
The hatred was gone.
Love pierced her heart.
There was no reason to go on.

Molly's pups shared a feeling.
One Charlee knew she didn't deserve.
"We're all just hounds," Patches said
"None are better. None are worse."
"Some come from breeders,
some come from shelters."
"Some are different,
but none are first."

Molly watched from nearby,
But not too close to be seen.
She smiled to herself.
Charlee no longer had to be mean.

Frederick's words made the difference.
The old bully was not who
people thought he should be.
But he changed Charlee's life
and the pups you could see.

There's a message of love
as we consider this hound.
Frederick's heart ruled over those
who cast him down.

A bully is not how you're born,
but how you act.
And remember it well
as you consider this fact.

Whether purebred or stray,
whether pretty or with fleas.
Love your hound
tan, red or brown
and you'll get more in return
you'll see.

OUR HEROES

Steven Nogueria	Susan Clarich	Richard Greene
Jean Marie Schiraldi	Mary Ann Litchfield	Sarah Alion
Chelsea J. Carter	Jim Proeller	Jane Ruetze
Carolynn Utiger Clarida	Eulogia Damer	Suzanne Austin
Corrie Pappas	Katherine Bennett	Terry Giarrosso
Kim Cate	Jill P. McMahon	Schildroth
Becky Thumma	Catherine Shoichet	Michael Barmish
Brooke Binkowski	Mary Jo Merkowitz	Milan Sekulic
Sarah Anthill	Kathi Franciscus	Nicole Kleinberg
Tricia Fox	Windy Thompson	Tammy Davis
Jeanine Coombs Todd	Linda Bevard	George Sekulich
Erin O'Keeffe	Martha Johnson	Zarifmo
Terry Irving	Chris LaGesse	Genii Sidoli
Lisa Bishop	Kerry Burner	Bill & Janice
Susan Cicero	Jennifer Noble	Staton
Phil & Susan Gast	Saeed Ahmed	Pete Beck
L. Deason	Warren Fried	Stephanie Oswald
Matt Smith	J. DiBenedetto	
Christine Kljajic	Kate King	

ABOUT THE AUTHOR

Ed Payne is a veteran broadcast and digital journalist with more than 30 years in the business. Millions have read his stories on CNN.com. You can also hear his voice on TV reports for the network and on hundreds of CNN affiliates across the United States. "Molly and the Bully - The Daily Rounds of a Hound 2" is his second children's book.

ABOUT THE ILLUSTRATOR

Britt Sekulic is a freelance illustrator and graphic designer based in Los Angeles. In addition to "Molly and The Bully," you can see more of her illustrations in the children's books "Come Along and Dream" and "The Daily Rounds of a Hound" as well as various design work at brittsekulic.com.

Made in the USA
Charleston, SC
03 February 2015